Margaret Hillert's

The Cow That Got Her Wish

Hey, diddle, diddle,
The cat and the fiddle,
The cow jumped over the moon;
The little dog laughed
To see such sport,
And the dish ran away with the spoon.
—Mother Goose

A Beginning-to-Read Book

Illustrated by Linda Prater

DEAR CAREGIVER,

The books in this Beginning-to-Read collection may look somewhat familiar in that the original versions could have been a part of your own early reading experiences. These carefully written texts feature common sight words to provide your child multiple exposures to the words appearing most frequently in written text. These new versions have been updated and the engaging illustrations are highly appealing to a contemporary audience of young readers.

Begin by reading the story to your child, followed by letting him or her read familiar words and soon your child will be able to read the story independently. At each step of the way, be sure to praise your reader's efforts to build his or her confidence as an independent reader. Discuss the pictures and encourage your child to make connections between the story and his or her own life. At the end of the story, you will find reading activities and a word list that will help your child practice and strengthen beginning reading skills. These activities, along with the comprehension questions are aligned to current standards, so reading efforts at home will directly support the instructional goals in the classroom.

Above all, the most important part of the reading experience is to have fun and enjoy it!

Shannon Cannon

Shannon Cannon,
Literacy Consultant

Norwood House Press • www.norwoodhousepress.com
Beginning-to-Read™ is a registered trademark of Norwood House Press.
Illustration and cover design copyright ©2017 by Norwood House Press. All Rights Reserved.

Authorized adapted reprint from the U.S. English language edition, entitled The Cow That Got Her Wish by Margaret Hillert. Copyright © 2017 Margaret Hillert. Reprinted with permission. All rights reserved. Pearson and The Cow That Got Her Wish are trademarks, in the US and/or other countries, of Pearson Education, Inc. or its affiliates. This publication is protected by copyright, and prior permission to re-use in any way in any format is required by both Norwood House Press and Pearson Education. This book is authorized in the United States for use in schools and public libraries.

Designer: Lindaanne Donohoe
Editorial Production: Lisa Walsh

LIBRARY OF CONGRESS CATALOGING-IN-PUBLICATION DATA

Names: Hillert, Margaret, author. | Prater, Linda, illustrator.
Title: The cow that got her wish / by Margaret Hillert ; illustrated by Linda Prater.
Description: Chicago, IL : Norwood House Press, [2016] | Series: A beginning-to-read book | Originally published in 1982 by Follett Publishing Company. | Summary: "Inspired by 'The Cow Jumped Over the Moon,' Brownie the cow wants very much to jump over the moon and works hard to achieve her dream. Includes reading activities and a word list"-- Provided by publisher.
Identifiers: LCCN 2016001871 (print) | LCCN 2016022847 (ebook) | ISBN 9781599537979 (library edition : alk. paper) | ISBN 9781603579599 (eBook)
Subjects: | CYAC: Stories in rhyme. | Cows--Fiction.
Classification: LCC PZ8.3.H554 Cp 2016 (print) | LCC PZ8.3.H554 (ebook) | DDC [E]--dc23
LC record available at https://lccn.loc.gov/2016001871

288N—072016
Manufactured in the United States of America in North Mankato, Minnesota.

"I want to have fun,"
said Brownie, the cow.
"I want to have fun—
and I think I know how."

"There once was a cow
that jumped over the moon.
That's what I want to do,
and I'll start right at noon."

"Why, a cat can't play
the fiddle.
It can't play a tune.
And a silly old cow
can't jump over the moon."

"Oh, no," said her friends.
"If you try such a jump,
    do you know what will happen?
    You're sure to go BUMP."

"And besides," they all said,
"you can't do it at noon!
Way up in the sky
you can't see any moon."

The cow was not happy.
She ate and she sat.
She sat and she ate
and she waited and sat.

"I'll wait till the sun sets,
and then very soon,
I know I'll be up, up,
and over the moon."

"I will go for a walk."

"I will climb up a hill
and jump over the moon.
Yes, I will. Yes, I will."

"I think I can make it.
Just look at me jump.
One, two, three. Here I go.
I go up, up, and—

BUMP!"

"Now, look," said her friends.
"Here's a lump and a hump.
What a silly old Brownie
to think you can jump."

"But I want to, I want to,
I want to, I say.
I know I can do it.
I'll find a good way."

"I'm tired," said Brownie.
"I sit and I sit.
I never have fun.
Not a bit. Not a bit."

"I know what I'll do.
I will try a balloon.
I'm sure that will help me
jump over the moon."

"A big, big balloon
is the thing that I need
to get over the moon.
Yes, indeed.
Yes, indeed."

"Up, up, I will go now.
Up, up, I will jump.
This balloon is a help.
Here I go. Here I—

BUMP!"

A little raccoon
who sat on a stump
said, "I'll help you.
I'll help you
to make that big jump."

"Just look over here.
Do you see what I see?
Here's the moon
round and yellow
and big as can be."

"If you take a big run,
if you make a big jump,
you'll go over the moon,
and you will not go BUMP."

So the brown and white cow
took a run and a jump.
And she made it! She made it
without any BUMP.

"I did it!
I did it!
Oh, thank you, raccoon,
for now I'm the cow
that jumped over the moon."

Foundational Skills

In addition to reading the numerous high-frequency words in the text, this book also supports the development of foundational skills.

Phonological Awareness: The diphthong /ou/ sound

Oral Blending: Say the sounds of the following words separately and ask your child to listen to the sounds and say the whole word:

/k/ + /ou/ = cow	/n/ + /ou/ = now
/h/ + /ou/ = how	/h/ + /ou/ + /l/ = howl
/d/ + /ou/ + n = down	/gr/ + /ou/ + l = growl
/b/ + /ou/ = bow	/b/r + /ou/ + /n/ = brown
/cl/ + /ou/ + n = clown	/pl/ + /ou/ = plow
/t/ + ou/ + /n/ = town	/ch/ + /ou/ = chow

Phonics: The letters o and w

1. Demonstrate how to form the letters **o** and **w** for your child.
2. Have your child practice writing **o** and **w** at least three times each.
3. Write down the following words and ask your child to underline the letters **ow** in each word:

cow	Brownie	now	how	plow
brown	howl	growl	bow	down
chow	town	vow	crown	scowl

Fluency: Shared Reading

1. Reread the story to your child at least two more times while your child tracks the print by running a finger under the words as they are read. Ask your child to read the words he or she knows with you.
2. Reread the story taking turns, alternating readers between sentences or pages.

Language

The concepts, illustrations, and text help children develop language both explicitly and implicitly.

Vocabulary: Day and Night

1. Write the words **Daytime** and **Nighttime** on two pieces of paper.
2. Ask your child to draw pictures of several things he or she does at night and during the day on each paper.
3. Label each picture. Read each label and ask your child to repeat it.
4. Ask your child to read each label.
5. Give your child a clue about each picture, without using its name, and ask your child to point to the correct picture/label.

Reading Literature and Informational Text

To support comprehension, ask your child the following questions. The answers either come directly from the text or require inferences and discussion.

Key Ideas and Detail

- Ask your child to retell the sequence of events in the story.
- Why couldn't the cow jump over the moon at noon?

Craft and Structure

- Why did the cow have trouble jumping over the moon?
- Why do you think the author chose to write this story in rhyme?

Integration of Knowledge and Ideas

- Think of something you had trouble doing. Who helped you?
- Have you read other books where the words rhyme? Which ones?

The Cow That Got Her Wish uses the 127 words listed below.

This list can be used to practice reading the words that appear in the text. You may wish to write the words on index cards and use them to help your child build automatic word recognition. Regular practice with these words will enhance your child's fluency in reading connected text.

a	fiddle	jump(ed)	play	take	wait(ed)
all	find	just		thank	walk
and	for		raccoon	that('s)	want
are	friends	know	right	the	was
as	fun		round	then	way
at		little	run	there	what
ate	get	look		they	white
	go	lump	said	thing	who
balloon	good		sat	think	why
be		made	say	this	will
besides	happen	make	see	three	without
big	happy	me	sets	till	
bit	have	moon	she	tired	yellow
brown	help		silly	to	yes
Brownie	her	need	sit	took	you
bump	here('s)	never	sky	try	you'll
but	hill	no	so	tune	you're
	how	noon	soon	two	
can	hump	not	start		
can't		now	stump	up	
cat	I		such		
climb	I'll	oh	sun	very	
cow	I'm	old	sure		
	indeed	on			
did	if	once			
do	in	one			
	is	over			
	it				

ABOUT THE AUTHOR Margaret Hillert has helped millions of children all over the world learn to read independently. She was a first grade teacher for 34 years and during that time started writing books that her students could both gain confidence in reading and enjoy. She wrote well over 100 books for children just learning to read. As a child, she enjoyed writing poetry and continued her poetic writings as an adult for both children and adults.

Photograph by Glenna Washburn

ABOUT THE ILLUSTRATOR Growing up in Alabama, Linda Prater studied art at Auburn University, where she earned her Fine Arts degree. After graduating, she honed her skills as an artist and designer working at a variety of design and greeting card studios. Upon visiting Colorado, she was allured by the beautiful surroundings and decided to make it her home. She now works out of her home studio there and creates colorful, fun artwork.